BECKY TIRABASSI

Books in the **Today's Heroes** Series

BECKY TIRABASSI

by Becky Tirabassi

ZondervanPublishingHouse
Grand Rapids, Michigan

A Division of HarperCollinsPublishers

Becky Tirabassi
Copyright © 1994 by Rebecca A. Tirabassi

Requests for information should be addressed to:
Zondervan Publishing House
Grand Rapids, Michigan 49530

Library of Congress Cataloging-in-Publication Data

Tirabassi, Becky, 1954–
   Becky Tirabassi / by Becky Tirabassi
      p. cm. – (Today's heroes)
    ISBN 0–310–49651–9 (softcover)
     1. Tirabassi, Becky, 1954–   —Juvenile literature.
2. Christian biography—United States—Biography—
Juvenile literature. 3. Alcoholics—United States—
Biography—Juvenile literature.
[1. Tirabassi, Becky, 1954– . 2. Alcoholics. 3. Christian
life.] I. Title. II. Series.
BR1725.T57A3   1994
248.8'6'092–dc20
[B]
                                           94–36544
                                                CIP
                                                AC

All names have been changed to protect the privacy of the people involved.

Edited by Dave Lambert
Interior illustrations by Win Mumma
Cover design by Mark Veldheer
Cover illustration by Patrick Kelley

Printed in the United States of America

94 95 96 97 98 99/ LP /10 9 8 7 6 5 4 3 2 1

Contents

Chronology of Events

December 5, 1954. I am born in Berea, Ohio.

July 4, 1970. I get drunk for the first time.

September 1972. I leave Berea to move to Wisconsin.

March 1973. I begin college at Bowling Green State University.

May 1974. I drop out of college.

Labor Day, 1974. I leave for California.

July 17, 1976. I return to Cleveland to be in a wedding—and admit for the first time that I am an alcoholic.

August 26, 1976. I pray to receive Christ into my life.

October 1976. I leave California and return to Cleveland.

January 1977. I volunteer with Youth for Christ.

January 1978. I marry Roger Tirabassi, Executive Director of Cleveland Youth for Christ.

February 1979. I have my first and only child, Jacob Tirabassi.

February 1984. I make a commitment to pray for one hour a day.

December 5, 1984. I self-publish the first *My*

Partner Prayer Notebook; My Partner Ministries is born.

May 15, 1986. The Tirabassi family moves to Southern California.

January 1990. I begin my full-time speaking ministry and travel throughout the United States and Canada.

January 1992. My first fitness video, *Step into Fitness,* receives an Angel award and is ranked in the top nine fitness videos for 1992 by *Shape Magazine.*

June 9, 1994. I am a guest speaker at the Northeastern Ohio Billy Graham Crusade at the Cleveland Municipal Stadium.

1

The Fourth of July

I took my first drink on the Fourth of July when I was fifteen years old.

Just as we'd planned, I met my friends out at the lake near my hometown of Berea, Ohio. The sky was dark, and being in the woods was kind of scary, although we giggled and teased each other to hide it. We weren't old enough to buy our own beer, but we'd gotten hold of some and hidden it in the bushes earlier. Sure, we knew that drinking alcohol was wrong, but we also knew a lot of high-school kids who went drinking—and I was about to enter the exciting world of high school! I'd just graduated from ninth grade—junior high in our town.

Not that I felt all that confident about making the jump to high school. All through junior high, I had felt like I wasn't pretty enough or rich enough to be popular. I was a cheerleader, so at least during games and pep rallies people noticed me. Even so, I was very insecure.

We found the cans of beer and pulled them out. Most of my friends had just started drinking, and this was my very first time. To tell the truth, the beer was warm and didn't taste very good, but it was great just being together. We laughed and talked about everything from guys to school and friends.

Cindy, like me, was going to be in tenth grade. Sue and Trish were going into eleventh.

"I can't wait to get my driver's permit," I sighed. "Only a few more months until freedom!"

"You'll love it," Trish chimed in, "especially after school. You don't have to sit at home for hours!"

I took another sour swig of beer. "This is cool," I said, grinning. "I finally feel like a high schooler!"

Quickly, we became light-headed. After drinking all the beer we'd hidden, we walked—not too steadily—to the Fourth of July celebra-

Becky Tirabassi

tion and found many of our classmates in the same condition we were in.

Why did I take that first drink? Most of all, I wanted to be popular. I knew that at the time—but I didn't realize then that I had another reason—I was trying to escape some of my family problems. And I discovered in the weeks that followed that when I drank, I seemed funnier, happier, and carefree—until it wore off.

That first night I drank, I found myself talking to people I barely knew, but I wasn't shy or afraid of them like I was when I wasn't drinking. In fact, I talked loud, said hi to everyone, laughed a lot, and added a few swear words to my vocabulary—mostly because I thought it made me sound older.

We had planned ahead for this night. I'd gotten permission to sleep at my girlfriend Cindy's house. Her mom always went to bed before we got home, so we knew that we wouldn't get in trouble for coming in late or having beer on our breath. We even planned to sleep in the basement so we wouldn't have to get up early!

I had snuck in a few extra items before I left home that night to meet my friends. I brought mascara and blue eye shadow to put on after I left the house, because my mom didn't like me to wear any makeup at all. I wore a white blouse and blue jeans out of the front door but changed into jean shorts and a tank top at Cindy's house before we left for the park. And I even brought extra money in case something fun—like a Ferris-wheel ride—came up.

And everything happened just as we'd planned it.

As the fireworks ended in a splash of colors and loud, continuous booms, I was almost sad that the "party" was ending. For the first time, I felt confident and outgoing, even though I hadn't even started high school. My fears about fitting in and being accepted were forgotten—for a while. With two six-packs of beer in me, I finally felt happy!

"This was really fun, wasn't it?" I asked Cindy, who like me was experiencing the party scene for the first time.

"Absolutely great," she replied.

"Hey, Becky!" Trish called from where she stood with a group of girls. "Wanna go to Bob's Big Boy?"

Cindy and I had promised to stick together no matter what, so I looked to see what she wanted to do. She didn't seem too excited about Trish's offer. "Becky," she whispered, "why don't we just walk around and see if we can find some guys to talk to?"

"Okay," I agreed. I wanted fun more than food!

We left the fireworks and walked down Bridge Street toward Baskin-Robbins, our summer hangout. Our junior-high tradition was to get ice cream and sit around on the lawn with other kids our age. But tonight, before we got to the ice-cream parlor, a carload of senior football players pulled up to the curb. At our school, as at most schools, football players were heroes, and I knew who each one of them was.

"Hey, Becky!" they called out.

I almost fainted! They knew my name!

"Yeah?" I answered.

"Wanna cruise?" a guy named Jim asked.

One look at Cindy and I knew I wouldn't have to talk her into accepting *this* offer!

"Sure," I said. We ran up to the car; I hopped into the back seat and Cindy into the front.

Now I felt as if I were in the middle of a dream! Me—sitting next to a varsity football player, laughing and joking. And they seemed to even *like* me!

Someone handed me a cigarette. I'd never smoked before, but I wasn't about to let anyone know that, so I stuck it in my mouth and inhaled, hard. I almost choked. But I tried to stay cool, and the next puff was a little easier. I even tried

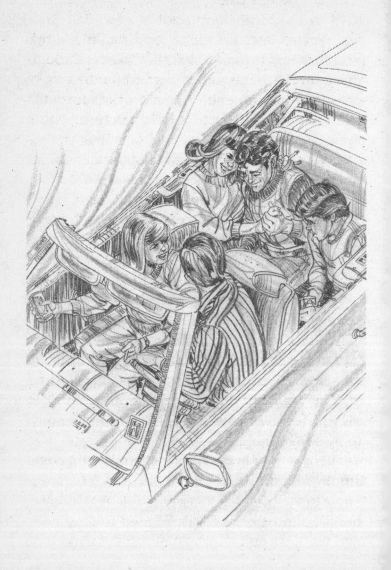

to blow a smoke ring!

I was sure packing a lot of new, first-time experiences into one night! And it all made me feel older, not so junior-highish. Cruising through the streets of Berea with important football players was an experience I would never forget. I promised myself that I would party like this again—soon.

"Hey, girls, where do you want to be dropped off?" the guys asked.

Immediately Cindy and I looked at each other, panicked. We loved being seen with these guys in town, but we couldn't have them drive us home because we were afraid to have our parents see us with them!

"How about driving us back to Baskin-Robbins?" I said.

Just before I got out of the car, one of those cute football players leaned over and kissed me—and I guarantee that he didn't kiss like one of the freshmen football players! *Yes,* I told myself, *we are definitely doing this again soon!*

That very night, we made plans for the next weekend—to hide our beer in the bushes behind the lake. Again.

2

Running Away

No matter how well you think you're hiding these things from your parents, they catch on. My mom didn't know that I was drinking, but she spotted signs of other trouble.

First, I changed my friends. In junior high, all of my friends were either cheerleaders, my neighbors, or other members of my swim team. But by the time I had been drinking for only a month, many of those friends were giving me a hard time because they didn't agree with the choices I was making. So what? Forget them! I already knew a lot of kids who wouldn't give me a hard time about drinking, because they were doing it too. I started to hang out with kids in the upper grades.

Another change my mom noticed was in my appearance. I went from the preppy cheerleader look to a hard, tough look—thick black eyeliner, frayed blue jeans, and sloppy, untucked T-shirts. I quickly gained weight from all the beers I drank each weekend—there are a lot of calories in those cans. Even my cheerleading skirt got tight. But I didn't care. That may sound hard to believe, but it's true—I really just didn't care. My attitude became rude and angry, my actions were mean and sneaky, I lied about where I was going and who I was going with, and my language grew more and more foul.

I even took up shoplifting as a "hobby." I didn't need to shoplift; my parents bought me clothes. But now I wanted different clothes from those they bought me. Besides, my new friends dared me. So I took some earrings, and even a dress!

By the summer after my sophomore year, I had started to hate living at home so much that I decided to graduate from high school a year early so that I could move out on my own that much sooner.

In fact, I wished I could leave home right

then. From the outside, my family looked normal. But now I hated normal. We went to church as a family *every* Sunday, as we had ever since I was a baby. My dad worked in a machine shop, and my mom sewed draperies to help pay for my older sister's college education.

My older sister, Reggie, was a very pretty blonde, liked by both teachers and students. But she was much older than me—she had started college when I went into first grade. My older brother, Rick, was five years ahead of me in school. He'd been the quarterback and captain of the high-school football team, and he'd dated the prettiest cheerleader.

But by the time I started junior high, my sister had gotten married and my brother had enlisted in the Air Force to fight in the Vietnam war. Being the only child at home was kind of lonely. And there was always a lot of yelling and screaming in my home. Because it had always been that way, it just seemed normal to me. Not that I liked it. Even before I started drinking, I never felt I could talk with my parents about my feelings or about my dreams—wanting to be a varsity cheerleader, going to college to be a physical education teacher. There always seemed to be a cloud of anger and unhappiness over our home.

My dad usually stopped at a bar every night before coming home for dinner. My mom would fix cocktails at 5:00 p.m. Drinking was a daily part of our family life—and it seemed to make everyone loud, quick-tempered, and unhappy. Once I got my driver's license, I didn't spend much time at home.

My mom agreed to let me graduate early. I think she had admitted to herself how difficult things were getting at home and thought things might settle down after I left for college. She made an appointment with the principal and asked him to work out my schedule to fulfill the requirements that I would need to finish high school in just one more year.

Mr. Deuchslander tried hard to talk me out of it. "Becky, aren't you going to miss being with the group of friends you've known since elementary school?" he asked.

"No," I answered coldly. The truth was, I didn't consider that group of kids my friends anymore. At times, we even acted like we hated each other.

"But what about cheerleading, which you like so much?"

"I don't care about that anymore," I lied. I *did* care—but it was too late. By that time, I'd gotten into so much trouble around school and

Becky Tirabassi

on the cheerleading squad with my drinking and smart mouth that, even if I tried out for varsity cheerleading, I doubted that I'd make it.

The sad fact was that high school had turned into a real drag. It didn't hit me at the time that the high-school experience I had looked forward to all through junior high was being ruined by the very choices I thought would make it better for me.

Drinking wasn't enough after awhile. I needed two six-packs of beer just to get a "buzz" or to feel "high." When a few of my partying friends started smoking marijuana, I quickly joined in. I never thought that alcohol or marijuana could hurt me. Using those things was hurting my friendships and family relationships, but like most users I was blind to that—I just thought everybody else was behaving like jerks. I didn't really notice how easily I could lie or swear. I didn't admit to myself how often I was blacking out and passing out when I drank. And of course, I thought "everyone was doing it"—or at least everyone that counted. I still thought that I was *just having fun!*

But at home, my fights with my mother grew louder and more frequent. I would even use swear words when I talked to her. And I argued about going to church—I just didn't want to go.

Running Away

Becky Tirabassi

"Becky!"

My mother's voice cut through my drowsing. *It couldn't be time to get up yet*, I thought. *I just got into bed.* My head pounded with the hangover from last night's partying. What time had I gotten to bed? I had no idea. I couldn't even remember coming home—something that was happening more and more often lately.

"Becky! It's almost time to leave for church! Get out of bed and get dressed! You're already too late to eat breakfast!"

Breakfast—yuck! Just the thought of food turned my stomach. I rolled over and moaned and pulled the covers over my head. Mom sounded angry—she'd probably been calling me for a long time. Well, tough. I felt lousy. Why hurry out of bed to get dressed just to go to a church that had nothing to do with me anyway? Just because Mom wanted me to?

The door slammed open, and Mom stood in the doorway, hands on her hips. "Look at you!" she fumed. "Still in bed, and we have to leave in fifteen minutes! What time did you get home last night?"

"Just leave me alone," I grumbled. "I don't feel good. I need to sleep a little longer. You guys just go on."

"No!" she said. "Get up and get dressed *now!*"

"Mom," I said, getting angrier, "I said I don't feel good! You know I don't like to go to church anyway, and now you're going to make me go even when I'm sick? Forget it! I'm staying here."

"Oh, no, you're not!" Mom took a couple of steps toward me and pointed into my face. "You're going to church if I have to—"

"If you have to what?" I challenged her. By then my father had come to my bedroom door.

They looked at me, totally disgusted, and then said, "We don't even know you anymore, Becky." Their eyes seemed full of pity—or was it hate? "We'll be waiting in the car for you."

I threw on some clothes, combed my hair, brushed my teeth, and reluctantly got into the car. I hated every minute of being with them.

For one thing, they were too strict—or so I thought. They always said no to everything I wanted to do. I hated living at home.

At seventeen, I decided I'd had enough.

One Saturday night my parents went to a wedding. I had never invited my boyfriend to come over even when my parents were home— and for *sure* I wasn't allowed to have anyone over when they were gone. But I was tired of living under their rules, and I knew they'd be gone

Becky Tirabassi

all evening long—so I decided to have a little party.

Guess what? My parents forgot something and came back to the house to get it! My boyfriend and I were making out on the couch, after having had quite a bit to drink, but I wasn't too drunk to recognize the sound of my dad's key in the front-door lock. By the time he flipped on the light switch, I had jumped up and was standing in the middle of the living room, yelling at him. But he yelled back just as loudly, and then he made my friends leave.

I ran into my bedroom and slammed the door. I was so angry—not because I'd done something wrong, but because I'd been caught! Drunk and embarrassed, I wanted to blame them.

I screamed from inside my bedroom, "I hate you!" And I meant it. "I can never bring people here! You always embarrass me!" I sobbed, falling onto my bed. I hated my life.

After everything quieted down and I was sure my parents had gone to bed, I lifted the window and slipped out. I ran to my girlfriend's house, and all my friends were there. I never called home to tell my parents where I was. If they were worried—good! I *wanted* them to miss me. I *wanted* to hurt them.

That was the first time I ran away, but it definitely wasn't the last.

Every few months, my drinking or lying or rebellious attitude would get me into some kind of trouble. And every time I would run away. Each time I would stay away a longer time than before, my heart would grow harder and more filled with hate, and my relationship with my parents would grow more distant.

At seventeen years old, a year before all my childhood friends, I graduated—without going to my own senior prom or even trying out for varsity cheerleading. Being a varsity cheerleader had been my childhood dream. But I had given up all my dreams—just so I could party.

Becky Tirabassi

3

Leaving Home at Seventeen

All of my buddies were going off to college. As brave and bold as I appeared on the outside, on the inside, I was afraid. Moving out of the house, starting a new life for myself somewhere else—it sounded great to me, but it was also a big step—a frightening big step. Because of those fears, I kept putting off the decision about which college to attend. I kept putting it off, and putting it off—until finally August rolled around, and it was too late to enroll anywhere.

Again, a dream seemed to be slipping away from me.

But I couldn't stand to see all of my friends driving away and leaving me behind, so I made an impulsive decision that would at least get me out of town. I called my older sister and asked if I could live with her in Madison, Wisconsin. In a few short weeks, the plans were made and I was about to leave home—officially—for the first time.

And, hey—that sounded like a good reason to celebrate! All of my girlfriends got together and had a "Good-bye Cheech" party for me. My nickname at the time was Cheech, after half of the movie/comedy team, Cheech and Chong—a nickname chosen because I was the biggest partyer of us all. I didn't know then that this attribute of mine—being able to drink more than anyone else—was a sign of alcoholism. My blackouts (not knowing what you're saying or doing even though to other people you seem to be awake) and passing out (falling asleep wherever you are because you have too much alcohol in your system—even if you're driving or talking to someone) should have been warning signs to me, but I ignored them. I had the same mistaken belief that many kids have: that only old men who sleep on the streets, can't hold a job, smell like whiskey, and drink in the morning are alcoholics. I believed that kids who drank were only having fun!

We all went our separate ways in September. Most of my friends went to Ohio colleges, while I went off to Wisconsin. But I was still sad. Things would never be the same, I knew. My girlfriends would meet a guy or join a sorority and start a whole new life around their new friends—and Becky, the one who wasn't even going to college, would be left out.

In Wisconsin, my loneliness looked for company, and I continued to drink. That December, I turned eighteen. Liquor laws in Wisconsin were different. They served all types and strengths of alcohol—beer, wine, and the hard stuff—to anyone eighteen or older.

It was a whole new world! I'd never had any real problem getting alcohol before, even when I was underage. There was always a way. But now I was legal! Suddenly, instead of a hidden keg at somebody's house, I lived in the world of cocktail lounges, sloe gin fizzes, and scotch on the rocks. One way or another, I drank almost every day—and this time I didn't have to use a fake I.D. I didn't have any real friends in Wisconsin yet. But when I was drinking in a bar or a lounge, I immediately had something in common with the strangers around me—we were all drinking.

So that I could be totally independent, I started working at an insurance company, which gave me enough income to move into an apartment with a girl I had met, Mary, a senior at the nearby University of Wisconsin. My friends from the office often went drinking after work, and naturally I went with them. That then turned into drinking binges over the weekends. I soon fell into the same pattern I'd established back in Ohio: Each time I drank, I seemed to get into more trouble than the time before—trouble like being late to work or getting caught in a lie about where I was. And at my company's Christmas party at a fancy restaurant, I made a total fool of myself. I was so drunk that I fell into the coat racks and lost my glasses. And that was a serious problem, because I can barely see without my glasses, and so there was no way I could drive home (not that I should have tried it anyway, in my condition).

One of the company vice presidents offered to drive me home. *That's awfully nice of him,* I thought, *to drive me home when he probably has more important people he could be spending his time with. He's such a nice guy.*

Unfortunately, he wasn't being as nice as I'd thought. He just figured that this would be a perfect opportunity to take advantage of me. He

Becky Tirabassi

probably thought I was so drunk I wouldn't even know what he was doing—or remember it later.

As he drove, he threw an arm around me and pulled me close to him. I started feeling sick—sick from too much drinking and because this forty-year-old married man with kids was just about to put "the moves" on me. When he sensed my resistance, he stopped at another bar, probably thinking that a few more drinks would loosen me up. In fact, they made me more nauseated. He finally gave up on me and took me home.

By the time he pulled his car up to my apartment, I couldn't even walk. He had to carry me to the door and ring the bell. Mary, my roommate, dragged me into the bathroom and threw me into the bathtub to try and sober me up. It took a long time—and my hangover lasted two days.

I showed up at the office on Monday morning, but I was so embarrassed and ashamed of myself I was afraid to look anybody in the eye. *Will they ever forget what a fool I made of myself?* I wondered. *Will they remember, every time they look at me, how I looked crawling around on my hands and knees under the coat rack in the restaurant, my clothes a mess, looking for my glasses?*

I couldn't get those thoughts out of my

mind, and I actually became so ashamed that I decided to leave Wisconsin to escape that embarrassment. Besides, the more I thought about it, the more I disliked my "independent" life. I had to buy my own food and clothes, pay rent and utilities—surely life would be easier somewhere else.

I called home. "Mom, what do you think about me starting college spring quarter at Bowling Green State University?" I'd thought this over beforehand, and I didn't really think she'd go for it. After all, she'd seen me mess up all through high school, so she'd probably figure college would be a waste of time and money for me. I threw out my strongest arguments: "I've saved enough money to pay for the quarter myself, so you wouldn't have to pay anything. And I'd really be ahead of my age group, and only a little behind my friends. Besides, I'd be closer to home."

There was a pause, and then she answered, "Yes, Becky, you can go to Bowling Green next semester if you want to." But I could hear in her tone of voice what she really thought—that I would mess up that opportunity just like I had so many other things.

Becky Tirabassi

4

College Confusion

All through high school, I'd had a pretty romantic picture of what college life would be like—unlimited freedom, a great dorm room, just a bunch of wild and crazy kids in a nonstop party.

Then I moved into a dorm at Bowling Green, and it wasn't like that at all—not even close. In fact, it was almost like living in somebody else's home under a whole new set of rules that weren't any better than my dad's rules—just different. There were curfews and shared shower rooms, too few televisions, plenty of homework, and you *still* had to do your own laundry!

But my greatest disappointment was my roommate. She was exactly the opposite of me. She was a neat, super-organized honor student who never drank or partied. And even worse, she dressed like a nerd from the fifties with a ponytail, white sneakers, and blue jeans that were too short! By the end of the semester's first week, I was absolutely miserable.

She must have been a good influence on me, though. At the end of my first quarter at Bowling Green, I had a straight-A report card—despite my party-hardy habits.

Because I'd been drinking every day before coming to BGSU and because many of my high-school partying friends attended BGSU too, I had immediate drinking partners. Dorm life may have been a disappointment, but my expectation that college would be one huge party wasn't far off.

I drank on Monday nights with "the girls," because our college bars had Ladies' Night—two drinks for the price of one for girls. Tuesday was Couples' Night—and I could always find a buddy to join me. Then on Thursday night came the traditional campus Happy Hour. And for nights when there was no special occasion, I stocked six-packs of beer in my own dorm-room refri-

Becky Tirabassi

gerator to have anytime I pleased with anyone I wanted!

And each night I drank, I either blacked out or passed out, then woke up the next morning hung over. Despite that obvious pattern, I *still* didn't think I had a drinking problem! I thought everyone who was "cool" was doing just what I was doing.

The party didn't end when I moved back home for the summer. I got a job so I'd have some money to party with, and then tried to make up for lost time with my old friends. Because we were all out of school, Pam and a bunch of girls got together each night after work at the local bar to dance and drink. Sometimes we'd go over to another friend's house to smoke marijuana.

Smoking pot was something we were doing pretty regularly now. It usually made us lethargic, moody, and slow—just the opposite of the way alcohol made me feel, so it was a strange mixture. It wasn't my favorite way to party, but it was a cheap high.

I spent plenty of time with my friends that summer, because home was the last place I wanted to be. When I was there, I was nursing a hangover and listening to my mom's nagging at the same time. It's amazing that we survived the summer without one of us having a nervous breakdown.

In the fall I went back to BGSU, and it looked as if I'd have a better time this year. At least I had a roommate who liked to hang out with my friends. The only problem was that she was also really pretty, thin, had a lot of money, and drank very little—all of which made me very jealous of Connie. She was so well liked by the guys that I constantly felt second-best. In fact, because of my beer drinking, I had gained so much weight that I had to buy a larger size in clothes than I'd ever had before. Being around such a "perfect" roommate made me envious of her and angry at myself. And what was the solution to that? Have another beer.

During that fall quarter Connie and I traveled down to Champaign to stay with some of my high-school friends for the University of Illinois's homecoming celebration. I got to the campus early—mid-afternoon on Friday—to get the earliest possible start on two straight days of partying.

Later that afternoon several of us girls were sitting in a dorm room, waiting for Pam's roommate Dawn to finish dressing for our night on the town. Dawn paused in the middle of applying her mascara and reached into a dresser drawer.

Becky Tirabassi

Pulling out a small vial of pills, she asked, "You ever try Quaaludes, Becky?"

"No," I said, game for anything. "What'll it do?"

"Everything slows down," she said. "Like slow motion. And then you'll laugh and laugh. Try one."

So I took it and waited for something to happen. "How long does it take?" I asked after a few minutes.

"Depends," Dawn answered. "Usually not long. Aren't you feeling anything?"

"I don't think so."

We left for town. By the time we reached the first bar, I decided the Quaalude wasn't going to affect me and began downing beer until I was rip-roaring drunk. Then the Quaalude finally hit—and hit hard. I don't remember going back to the dorm.

I woke up very late the next morning, with such a bad hangover I had to drink a few beers to numb the pain enough to make the football game. I drank some more while I watched, and that evening went out for some serious partying.

As we piled into the car the next day to head home, Connie called out to Dawn, "Good-bye! We had a great weekend!"

I smiled and waved good-bye too, but as we

settled into the long drive home, I had to admit that I was disappointed. *A great weekend?* I asked myself. *What was so great about it? I don't even remember most of it. What did we do? Where did we go? What's the point of having fun if you can't even remember it afterward?*

Connie sounded like she'd had a great time, though, and she could even remember it. That made me even more jealous of her. The truth is, I'd have loved to be more like her—but my drinking seemed to separate us. When I drank, I became very loud and vulgar. Because she didn't drink very often or very much, she remained poised and in control no matter where we went. I used foul language; she rarely swore, always seeming like a "lady." And in the mornings she would look cute and fresh while I struggled with alcohol on my breath and smeared makeup on my face. And I almost always had a doozy of a hangover (shakes, headache, and nausea). Although we both knew lots of guys, I was "just one of the guys," while she was regularly asked out on dates! I was constantly comparing myself to her, but I wasn't strong enough to make any changes in myself to improve the things I didn't like.

One Saturday near the end of the winter quarter, I was invited to a big fraternity party.

Becky Tirabassi

The guests included a lot of people I didn't know from the University of Illinois who drank even harder and faster than most of my friends. As usual, I downed more than my share of beer. Rowdy music, good-looking athletes, loud jokes, spontaneous kissing—it all seemed like great fun. At first.

The night got even wilder when the fraternity guys began singing drinking songs with the crudest lyrics I had ever heard in my life. As the night turned into morning, I had more beers and shots of whiskey than I could count and began to feel very sleepy. Leaving the noise behind, I wandered around the old two-story house until I found an empty bedroom, climbed onto a pile of coats on the bed, and fell asleep.

I woke up slowly as someone roughly rolled me over. I opened my eyes to see a drunken guy with a wild grin standing over me. Then another guy's face came into focus, and I realized that what I was feeling was their hands on my body as they tried to take off my clothes!

Suddenly wide awake, I kicked at them and screamed for help. "Get away! Leave me alone!"

Now they were laughing. They weren't afraid of me. And they weren't about to stop. One of them pinned me down. My screams weren't much of a defense, and I was too weak and disoriented because of my drunkenness to fight them off.

Then the door burst open. A friend of mine stepped in and said, "Hey—what's going on?"

"Craig! Help me! Please! Help!" I screamed, struggling.

Reluctantly, the two guys who were attacking me let go. I jumped to my feet, pulled my clothes back into place, grabbed my coat, and ran out of the room, down the steps, and out the front door.

Stunned, embarrassed, and ashamed by what had almost happened, I ran back to my dorm room. Once I got behind the safety of my own door, I cried uncontrollably.

That may have been the first time I really saw what a mess my life had become. My grades were dropping from A's to C's, and I didn't have any real friends. Now I had to face this.

I felt more lonely and desperate than I had ever felt before. I knew that I couldn't just go on as if nothing had happened. Somehow I managed to sleep a little that night, but in the morning I got up and called home.

"I'm quitting school," I told my mom. "I want to come home." I couldn't bring myself to add "again."

There was a long silence on the other end of

Becky Tirabassi

the line before my mother, obviously thinking of how poorly things had gone last summer, asked, "How are we going to make it?"

"I'll be busy," I assured her. "I'll work downtown and take classes part-time at Cleveland State University. I'll have to study. Besides, I won't be around much. It won't be like before."

My mother sighed, "I don't know . . ."

"I'll change," I promised. "You'll see. I'll do whatever you want me to do. I'll get it together. I just want to come home."

Another long silence. "Okay."

So I packed up my things, bummed a ride back home with a friend, and never went back. I never even told Connie or my other suite mates that I was leaving. I left BGSU humiliated.

5

California Freedom

I worked full-time that summer—my third since high school—partly to make money and partly to keep out of the house. Despite my assurances to my mother, our relationship just kept getting worse, and I figured it was best for everybody if I were home as little as possible. I desperately wanted to get away from the pressures of college and the control of my family.

On one of our nightly binges, a few of my girlfriends and I dreamt about moving to California—the land of sandy beaches and blonde surfers! By the end of summer, the dreaming had turned into real plans.

My first step was to buy a car for the trip out west—my first car. I used the money I had saved from working, along with some I'd borrowed from my brother. On Labor Day of 1974, my friends and I packed up my Ford with stereos, clothes—and a few bags of pot hidden in the carpet. Dressed in jean shorts, halter tops, bandannas, and flip-flops, we waved good-bye to our hometown and pulled out onto the highway, feeling grown-up and free.

With maps and money, we headed off into the sunset to start a new life. I had formed the habit of drinking or smoking dope while driving, a habit I continued on the California trip to make the long hours on the road seem more fun—or at least I *told* myself that's why I was doing it. What I hadn't yet noticed was that, at some point along the line, my daily use of drugs and alcohol had switched from using them to "have fun" to *needing* them to feel normal. Every day, I would use something to change my mood from sad to happy or from anxious to calm. Addicted? *No way,* I thought. *All my friends drink and smoke dope, and so do I. No big deal. It's just normal. We do it to have fun.*

The lesson I'd learned at that fraternity

Becky Tirabassi

party when two guys had tried to rip my clothes off hadn't lasted long.

In California, we rented an apartment on the top of a hill by a community college. Each of us found full-time jobs, and together we'd go out nightly to dance and drink. Even when money was low and there were bills to be paid and nothing in the refrigerator, I still somehow had enough money to party. My life revolved around—depended upon—getting high.

My first job was in an office in downtown Monterey. It was a fun place to work, because a lot of the people who worked there were close to my age and liked to party. But it didn't pay me enough to cover the rent plus car payments, food, and clothes. A couple of times I even had to write home for loans to pay bills, and that upset me. I wanted to be independent.

Then I heard about another job, at the local Chevrolet dealership, that seemed to have a lot of room to move up the ladder. I really wanted the job, so when I was interviewed by a very beautiful and professional woman, I pretended to be a very "put-together" nineteen-year-old. Even though I was concentrating hard on making a good impression, I couldn't help but admire the business manager who was interviewing me, Mrs. Carros. She was beautifully dressed in an expensive outfit, and her red hair was cut in a perfect style for her. I got the job—and working with Mrs. Carros every day, my admiration for her grew. She was always dressed in the latest styles, and she wore different jewelry every day. She was "the boss"—and even the men who worked for her knew it. She was self-controlled and very smart.

For the first few months at that job, trying to make a good impression on her, I hid my bad habits, such as swearing and smoking. She never knew that on my lunch hours I would have a beer or smoke a joint with some of my coworkers. But as the months went on, living a double life—being one person on my own time and pretending to be someone else at work—became too difficult.

And it wasn't just Mrs. Carros I was trying to fool. I had moved out of my apartment and into my Aunt Martha and Uncle Tim's house to save money, and they had no idea how I lived when I was out of their sight.

But one night I blew it all. On my way home from drinking with my buddies at a bar, I blacked out and drove my brand-new Chevy off the road and into a parked car.

With my face and the front of my jacket covered with blood, I was rushed to a hospital—

before the police had even arrived at the accident scene. By the time they caught up to me, I had already been treated for my injuries (which, fortunately, were minor) at the hospital and released—and that's why I wasn't charged with drunk driving. Still, having to explain my accident to my boss and coworkers was humiliating. That and the loss of the new car I'd been so proud of shook me up enough that I quit drinking for a few months. But when my scars healed, I started drinking and partying again.

That's when I met John.

At first, we would meet for a few drinks after work. Then we began to eat dinner together every night, having wine or beer with our meals. Soon, I realized that I didn't want to leave him at night, and by that time I didn't see any reason that I should. Most nights, before going to bed, we would snuggle into a big chair in front of his fireplace and sip Cold Duck as the crackling fire slowly changed to glowing embers. On weekends, when we went hiking or canoeing or swimming at the beach, we always took a supply of beer or wine. Drinking was a big part of what we did when we were together.

As the weeks rolled by, I felt more convinced than ever that John was my fairy-tale prince. In all my previous relationships, I'd been

Becky Tirabassi

the spontaneous one, the instigator, the leader. I didn't have to do that with John. He took charge, and I just enjoyed being swept along.

I never knew what to expect. Any night after work, he might be waiting for me with a picnic basket all packed. We would take a two-hour drive to Big Sur and eat a romantic supper seated on a blanket high on a bluff as we watched the sun set over the Pacific. Or he'd throw a couple of sleeping bags and a tent in the back of his pickup and announce, "We're going to sleep tonight under a redwood tree," and we'd be off for a weekend in the mountains.

One night, just about sunset, we were walking out of a bar when John said, "Wow, what a nice night. Hey—I've got an idea." The next thing I knew, he had rented a canoe and was paddling us out into Monterey Bay. We sat there watching the sun set.

Suddenly I heard a strange noise: *Arghf! Arghf!* Across the water, a short distance away, I saw a huge dark body swimming toward us. My heart almost stopped.

"John!" I screamed. "What is it?"

Seeing how frightened I was, John burst into laughter and pointed to the mustached face of a huge walrus, just a few feet from our canoe.

"They won't hurt us," he chuckled. "They're just curious."

I laughed, too—still nervous about the huge animals, but aware suddenly of just how much I liked every minute I spent with John. I'd never known anyone like him. *Don't lose him,* I told myself. *You'll never find another one like John.*

Before long, we moved in together. I knew it was wrong to live with someone you aren't married to—first of all, because my mother had raised me with very high moral standards, and secondly because, deep inside, I knew that sex outside of marriage was against God's laws. But those beliefs weren't strong enough to stop me from living with John.

I wanted to be loved. And I thought when you lived with someone, you would automatically feel happy and "in love." But the feelings I thought I'd feel—of love, security, and companionship—weren't the ones I felt living with my boyfriend. Instead, I was embarrassed to tell most people about it. Besides, the more I talked to John about making a real commitment to me—a "forever" kind of commitment—the more he felt trapped by me and the more he talked about needing his "freedom." Living with John, I felt guilty, ashamed, and miserable. Unable to

Becky Tirabassi

change him and not strong enough to move out, I drank more, took more drugs, lied about my life to most people, and grew more anxious and discouraged with every passing day.

6

"I'm an Alcoholic"

There she is! Hey, Becky!"

I heard their shouts before I'd even made it out of the walkway from the plane; all of my old friends had come to the airport to greet me. I was back home in Cleveland to be in my friend Kara's wedding. It was summer, and I'd just turned twenty-one.

I'd been looking forward to this trip for weeks, figuring it would be one great big high-school reunion and week-long party!

But I'd been worried, too, because John and I would be apart for almost a month this summer; John spent part of each summer backpacking in Canada. In fact, I had cried often as summer approached, afraid that our relationship was going to be different when we both returned to California. My greatest fear was that John would find another girlfriend, or that he would cheat on me with some cute girl he might meet. I just didn't trust him.

John had taken me to the airport to catch my flight to Cleveland that morning, and I had cried hysterically. As soon as I'd boarded the airplane, I had ordered a drink. By the time I stepped off the plane and met my friends, I was far from sober. We stopped at a couple of bars before we headed home, and I had several more drinks. More than once that night, I heard my friends laughingly say, "Same old Becky." And it felt good. *At last*, I thought, *I'm with people who accept me and love me the way I am.*

On the night of Kara's bachelorette party, one of my friends, Vicki, and I had finished off a fifth of vodka before seven o'clock. Then we talked everyone into heading downtown to our favorite bar for more drinks and dancing.

That's where I ran into George, a guy who was quite a bit older than me but who had gone to my high school. We danced together for a while and had a few more drinks, and then

Becky Tirabassi

someone suggested that we all drive out to the local quarry and go skinny-dipping. I didn't really feel like it, but if everyone else went, I figured I'd go along. Before we left, I had one more drink. That was the last thing I remembered until . . .

Wow, what a headache. I opened my eyes just enough to see where I was. There was a clock beside the bed I was in. It said 5:03. Was that AM or PM? Whose clock was that? Whose *bed* was this?

Confused but a little panicky, I sat up. I didn't recognize the room. Then I felt someone beside me.

At first I didn't recognize him because of the darkness. I leaned a little closer—and realized I was lying next to George!

I suddenly felt sick to my stomach. How had we gotten here? What had happened last night? I racked my brain, but it was no use—I couldn't remember anything after that drink at the bar. But it didn't seem likely that George had just offered me the use of his bed for the night out of the goodness of his heart.

My next thoughts were of John. I had promised him that I wouldn't sleep with another person, and less than two days later, *this* had happened! And to make matters worse, I had no idea what part of town I was in or where I'd left my car the night before. I wanted to just slip quietly away into the night, but I had no choice; I woke George up and asked him for a ride home.

I rode in silence, trying to recall something—anything—from the night before, but at the same time afraid to. This wasn't funny. This wasn't cute. This was disgusting.

I was in such emotional turmoil I kept thinking I was going to throw up. I asked myself over and over and over: *How? How did this happen?* But I didn't need to ask, because I already knew the answer: Every time I drank, I ran the risk of totally losing control of myself. It had happened before—when I'd wrecked my new Chevy, for instance. It had happened last night, making me feel cheap and disgusting. And it would happen again.

I had admitted to myself before that my life was totally messed up. But now, for the first time, I was forced to admit that I had a drinking problem. A *serious* drinking problem. There was no more denying it, no more hiding it.

George dropped me off at my parents' house. I walked up to the front door and slipped inside. By now it was a little after six. The first thing my bloodshot eyes focused on was my mother. Waiting for me to get home the night before, she'd fallen asleep on the couch.

Becky Tirabassi

She awoke as I tried to close the front door quietly behind me. "Becky?" She sat up. I expected her to explode. But she just sat there. Maybe she could tell by looking at me that she didn't need to say anything. Nothing she might have said could have made me feel any worse, any lower, or any more ashamed than I did at that moment.

Neither of us spoke as I walked over to an armchair facing the couch and sat down. After another long silence, I choked out the words no one ever wants to say: "Mom, I'm an alcoholic."

I had never said that before—never even thought it before that morning. But I knew it was true—and so did my mom.

We both began to cry. I rushed across the room and fell into her arms.

I sobbed so hard that I couldn't get any words out, but the painful thoughts of the previous night overwhelmed my mind. *What am I going to do now? How could I let this happen? How can I go on? What about John? I'm only twenty-one years old! What have I done to myself?*

Finally, exhausted, I walked back to my old bedroom and climbed into bed. There I pulled my knees up to my chin, closed my eyes, and covered my head with the sheet. I never wanted to face another day.

On Saturday night, I thought, *my friends will expect me to walk up that aisle at Kara's wedding and then go out with them afterwards and party my head off—and just be the "same old Becky." And I can't do it. I just can't do it.*

I wish I were dead.

7

The End of
the Old Becky

The rest of that week, I didn't drink a drop
of alcohol, in spite of my friends' prodding.
Sunday night, I returned to California. I knew I
had to face my boss and girlfriends and tell them
that I was an alcoholic, but even worse than
that—I would have to tell John when he got
home from his Canadian vacation.

With my body still on central time and my
emotions frayed after three-and-a-half days
without a drink, I went back to the apartment I

continued to rent with my friend Pam. Having two places allowed me to hide from my relatives the fact that I lived with John. John was out of town and she wasn't there, so I went to bed.

I don't know what time it was when I heard the apartment door slam shut. "Pam?" I called. I heard her bump into something in the living room, then a minute or two later her silhouette appeared in my doorway.

"Becky, you're home!" She sounded surprised. "I'm sorry—I was supposed to pick you up at the airport, wasn't I? I forgot you were coming."

"Can you come into my room for a minute?" I mumbled. "I need to talk."

Pam walked in and sat on the edge of my bed. "What's up, Beck?"

I took a deep breath. I had to tell someone. "Pam, I want you to know—I think I'm an alcoholic."

"No, you aren't," she laughed.

"I think I am."

"You are not. Okay, so maybe you drink too much. Just slow down!"

"I'm serious, Pam."

"No way are you an alcoholic!" She flounced off to bed.

Becky Tirabassi

I couldn't sleep. I don't know what I'd been expecting from Pam, but that wasn't it.

The next few weeks were almost unbearable. I tried to quit drinking completely, and my body reacted this time with shivers, nausea, sweating, and the feeling that I was going to break into pieces. (Those sensations are the effects of going off drugs and alcohol, called "withdrawal.")

Trying to explain my problem to my roommate hadn't worked—in fact, she took me to a party a few days later and kept after me to have "just one drink" until I finally gave in—and woke up the next morning with a horrible hangover. I learned the hard way that an alcoholic can't take "just one drink."

Telling my boss and friends why I couldn't drink was even more difficult. I was afraid to say the words "I'm an alcoholic" to them—after all, maybe they wouldn't like me anymore. Instead, I told them, "I think I have a drinking problem." But my friends didn't take me seriously; they reacted just as Pam had. And my boss, although she was sympathetic, had nothing helpful to offer. I needed more than a kind voice and a pat on the back—I needed some practical, concrete help in getting through the day without alcohol.

After three weeks of trying to quit drinking,

I had no more strength to fight the battle of my alcoholism. I felt like giving up on life. *I'm going to fail,* I thought. *I'm going to give in and go right back to drinking. I don't want to—I know I'm destroying myself. But I don't know how to fight it.*

On August 26, 1976, I was scheduled to appear at a court hearing for the car accident I had been in a year earlier. And I was really afraid. I knew I had to face the consequences for my actions, but I felt alone, scared to death of what might happen in the hearing, and disappointed in myself. I felt hopeless.

The long drive there forced me to think over the past six years. And I didn't like what I saw. *Why can I see things so much more clearly now?* I wondered. *Just because I haven't had a drink in a month?* For whatever reason, I was able to see my life as it really was—a mess. I could no longer run from my past—or my present.

I stood at the door to the courtroom that day, took a deep breath—and made a decision. I would face the future without lying. Lying had become just one more bad habit. And today was a perfect time to tell the truth—and then face the consequences, whatever they might be. I knew it wouldn't be easy.

Becky Tirabassi

But before the hearing, I had to talk to my lawyer. We sat in his office as he told me what to expect—and gave me a stern warning. Leaning toward me, his eyes intense and his finger tapping the desk to emphasize his point, he said, "Rebecca, if you lie on the stand, you'll be crucified!"

The fear and nausea I'd been feeling doubled. *Crucified?* I thought. *I only know of one person who's ever been crucified, and that's Jesus.* Why my lawyer chose those words, I'll never know, but they turned my thoughts in the right direction—toward God. The simple truth was, that day I had nowhere else to turn except to God. I needed help, and there was nowhere else I could turn to get that help. Somehow I knew that I needed to give my life to him. But how?

Then I thought of someone I could ask. On the previous Easter Sunday, I'd gone to church—certainly not a normal activity for me, but hey, it was Easter. I had ended up meeting and talking for a while with the janitor of that church. *He was kind of a strange guy, though,* I remembered. *What was his name? Oh, yeah—Ralph.* I also remembered something he had told me in our brief conversation that day: "Becky," he had said, "Jesus loves you just the way you are!" At the time, I'd been turned off by that "Jesus" talk. *Besides,* I'd thought at the time, *this guy has no idea just how bad a person I am! How can he be so sure Jesus will love me just the way I am?* But now just thinking about Jesus loving me gave me hope.

And hope was something I desperately needed. During the past month, starting even before that horrible morning with George and my discovery that I was an alcoholic, my feelings had gone far beyond just hating myself. I was seriously thinking of ending my life. Now, remembering Ralph's words, I saw a ray of hope that maybe my life could change—the first hope I'd felt in a long, long time.

The moment the court hearing ended, I jumped into my car and drove down Highway 1. I was heading for the church where Ralph the janitor worked. It's a beautiful drive; the highway curves along the ocean. But I was crying too hard to see it, and thinking too hard to be aware of the beauty. I had no idea what to expect when I found Ralph; I just knew I had to find him.

I was so desperate that when I pulled into the church parking lot, I slammed on the brakes and screeched to a halt. I jumped out of the car and ran down the steps to the church basement. *This is the end of my life as I've always known*

Becky Tirabassi

it, I thought. *This is the end of the old Becky. I don't know what's going to happen here, but I do know that when I walk out, I'll be a different person. This is the end of my addictions—and good riddance. I hate my life. I want out—now!*

At the bottom of the steps, I found Ralph getting ready to polish the floors of a children's Sunday school room. "Ralph!" I blurted out through my tears. "I need to talk!"

"No, Becky," he said calmly, seemingly not surprised that I was there, "we just need to pray."

I couldn't say yes fast enough.

"Do you want to ask Jesus to come into your life?" he asked.

"Oh, yes!" I cried.

So right there on those little kids' Sunday-school chairs, with my head bowed and my knees tucked up under my chin, I started my new life.

"I'll start out praying," Ralph explained, "and you just repeat after me and say the same things I say." He spoke slowly, so I wouldn't get lost: "Dear Jesus . . ."

But after Ralph got me started, he didn't need to lead me any longer. I knew what I needed to tell Jesus—that I was sorry. And I knew what I needed to ask him—to forgive me.

I prayed on and on, begging God for help in

every area of my life. Without holding back any secret or sin, I told God—and Ralph, who must have been awfully surprised by what he heard that day—about my whole messed-up life. I confessed every sin I could think of, and asked for forgiveness for what I'd done and for help not to repeat it in the future.

As I prayed, a steady calm came over me. I couldn't explain how, but I knew I felt a difference deep in my heart. As I confessed one sin after another, admitting my addictions and turning away from every aspect of my old, destructive life, my new peace changed slowly to joy, and through my tears I started to laugh.

I was actually talking to God! And he was *listening*—I could tell. He was with us in that room. He was listening to me, loving me, and forgiving me—even when I knew I didn't deserve it.

When I had finished listing all my sins, Ralph asked me to repeat after him again. "Jesus," he prayed, "come into my life; make me new."

Yes—that was *exactly* what I wanted. I needed—and wanted—to be a new person. "Come into my heart," I prayed, "and fill me to overflowing with an extra measure of your Holy Spirit, Lord, please."

And that's what happened.

As soon as we finished praying, Ralph

showed me a Scripture verse, 2 Corinthians 5:17, that says, "Therefore, if anyone is in Christ, he is a new creation; the old has gone, the new has come!" That was the greatest thing I could have heard, and I believed every word of it: By asking Jesus to come into my heart by faith, I had been given a fresh start, a new life, and no one would ever be able to take that away from me!

I was *not* going to go crazy! Instead, I was going to start over—with a brand-new life!

8

Starting Over, Helping Others

My whole life changed after that day!

First, a few days later, I found out that I would only be fined five dollars for my car accident, as it took place on a military base and not on public streets. I felt like a huge burden had been lifted from my shoulders. And I resolved to change my bad driving habits, as well as the rest of my life.

My friends, especially those I drank and partied with, found my "new life" hard to understand.

It seemed like an overnight change to them: One day they'd seen me drinking, and the next day I was telling them I couldn't even be around them or alcohol! We found we had little in common when we didn't drink together, and we soon drifted apart.

Harder for me to take was the reaction of my boyfriend, John. I had thought that he would be happy for me and my new life—after all, wasn't it obvious that this was better for me? Instead, he was upset. "You've changed too much!" he growled. "And why'd you move out of our house? We had a great thing going together."

"I just don't think it's right for us to be living together if we're not married," I answered. "I tried to convince myself it was okay before, but now that I've turned my life over to God—"

"That's another thing," he said, "all this God talk. You're just not the same Becky, and I don't like it. You're always reading the Bible—don't you realize how old-fashioned and out-of-touch the Bible is? There's nothing wrong with two people who love each other living together. But just because the Bible says it's wrong, you move out. You've moved back into the Dark Ages."

Not surprisingly, John and I soon found that we had nothing in common, either.

Now that I'd lost most of my friends and my

Becky Tirabassi

boyfriend, I felt alone in my "stand for Christ." I didn't like that feeling of loneliness—after all, it was my desire to fit in and be accepted and liked that had led me into the party life in the first place, and I still felt that need to have friends. And that was a danger for me. The best—and probably the *only*—way for me never to drink or even be tempted to drink again was not to be around alcohol, or even at a party where alcohol was served. I was willing to make that hard decision, but it would be a hard rule to keep if I yielded to the temptation to hang around with my circle of California friends.

I decided to go back home to Cleveland for a while until I grew stronger in my faith and in my decision to stay away from drugs and alcohol. There, I should be able to find some supportive, non-drinking friends.

My parents could hardly believe I was the same person. For the first time in six years, I didn't swear, drink, smoke, or lie to them. In fact, I couldn't stop talking about God. I even took my parents to church with me—and a few months later, they too asked Christ to come into their lives. It was very helpful to me for them to accept and understand my enthusiasm for God—and to share in it with me.

Once I settled into my old hometown, I

began to meet a lot of Christians who worked with high-school kids, sharing their faith in God at club meetings called Campus Life clubs. They belonged to an organization called Youth for Christ. I liked what I saw in their lives, and I liked what they were doing, so I volunteered to help. While training to be a youth worker and working as a staff member of the local Youth for Christ program, the director, Roger, became my best friend.

He was older than me, a stronger Christian, and a lot of fun. Most of all, he really loved God. It showed in the way he treated others, in his even temper, and in his generosity. After a year-long friendship, he asked me to marry him—and we had never kissed, or even dated!

After a short engagement, we had a big wedding with a lot of our friends as our brides-maids and ushers—twelve of them! Lots of the Campus Life kids and their parents came to our wedding on January 28, 1978—during one of the worst snowstorms to hit the Midwest in over a hundred years.

On our honeymoon, Roger and I were given a bottle of champagne by the airlines as a gift. Once we were at the hotel, Roger left our room for a few minutes—and I hurriedly popped the cork and downed two glasses of champagne.

When Roger came back, I guiltily told him what I'd done. Even though I'd been clean for almost a year, I still got tripped up sitting alone in a hotel room with a bottle of booze.

Roger listened to my confession, and then he said something that would become an important part of my recovery. "To help you stay away from this stuff," he said, motioning toward the half-full bottle, "I'll make a commitment never to take a drink of any alcohol again, for the rest of my life—or even have liquor in our home. And," he added, "I'll help keep *you* accountable never to take a drink."

Roger had never had a drinking problem, so I knew that his decision was for my sake. I also knew that, from that day on, I'd never have to be alone in my decision not to drink, nor would I have to feel pressure to drink if I was ever in a place where others were drinking, since Roger would be right beside me, saying no right along with me.

From that day, I have never had another drink. I've never even had the desire for one.

Ten days after our first wedding anniversary, on February 8, 1979, I had a little boy. We named him Jacob after my father and grandfather.

For the next eight years, Roger and I continued working together in Youth for Christ, where I was the Campus Life director and cheer-leading coach—at the same high school I had attended!

Roger and I loved our life—working together and helping high-school kids grow in their relationships with God and others. We had high-school students at our house nearly all the time—just to eat popcorn, watch TV, and have Bible studies.

One of those students was Steve. He loved to race BMX bikes, and before he even got his driver's license he and a bunch of his friends would ride their bikes over to our house after school.

We held weekly Bible studies for this rowdy bunch of guys in our living room, and afterwards we'd always move into the kitchen to talk and eat.

One night Steve stayed long after his friends had gone home, asking question after question about becoming a Christian.

That night, sitting at our kitchen table, Steve accepted Christ into his heart—with the help of some little illustrations that my husband made for him on a napkin. Steve took that napkin home and shared that same presentation with his younger brother David. David began to come to the Bible studies in our home, too, and soon he also accepted Christ. All through high school, these two brothers were our enthusiastic helpers, working hard to give their high school a big, fun, and exciting Campus Life club!

When Roger and I moved to California to become youth ministers at a large church, Steve kept in touch with us. Within a year, he got married and moved within fifteen minutes of us! A month later, he and his wife Lynn volunteered to help us with our youth group; later, they became our high-school staff members.

Last year, Steve was my son's junior-high pastor. We really felt that God was blessing us when Steve baptized Jacob. It's incredible to see how God works things out!

I'm not proud of the story of my drug and alcohol addiction, and of the mistakes I've made in life because of it. But, because my greatest desire has been to help others, especially students, see the dangers in drugs and alcohol, I have told that unpleasant story for one reason only: to help students see the "slippery slope" that drug and alcohol use leads to: physical and emotional dependence, the destruction of important relationships, and serious moral problems.

There are a lot of things you may be tempted to do over the next few years—drinking, smoking, drug use, sex, swearing, running with gangs, or even starving or overeating as a way to make yourself feel better or run from your problems. "Everybody's doing it," you may find yourself saying. But I tried most of those things—tried them and then pursued them, hoping that they would bring me satisfaction and happiness. I can tell you from experience that you won't find in those things what you are looking for. Stay away from them. Instead, lean on God when you feel lonely, unhappy, unloved, or unaccepted. You'll live a happier and healthier life—no doubt about it.

Through all of my struggles, I have found that God is the one who loves us most, forgives us always, and truly has a plan for our lives—a plan to help us out of trouble and then to set our feet on the path toward a life full of purpose and love.

Becky Tirabassi

9

Spiritually and Physically Fit

Eight years after that frantic prayer with Ralph in that church basement in California, I became so busy "serving God" that I no longer spent time *with* him. I taught three Bible studies a week, ran a Campus Life group, and met with kids one on one. Because of my busy life, I had slipped into the bad habit of reading my Bible and praying in bed late at night. I only talked to God when I had an urgent request, and I rarely listened to him. In short, I lost some of my zeal for God.

To recapture that fire, I made a decision to spend time with God *every day*—to talk with him in prayer (I find it helpful to write my prayers down) and then to listen to his answer (by reading my Bible). This daily habit, which I call my quiet time, has been the greatest help in keeping me out of trouble.

In fact, the first people I taught to journal (write) their prayers were high-school kids. In 1984, those kids helped me put together the *Quietimes Student Prayer Notebook*. It's available now as a paperback journal where you can write your prayers every day and keep a record of God's answers. It's not only a place for asking God for things—that's just one part of prayer. The *Quietimes Student Prayer Notebook* gives you a place to tell God that you love him (the *Praise* section), to say you're sorry for the wrong things you've done (in the *Admit* section), to list your prayer *Requests* (being sure to *ask* God and not *tell* him), and to thank him (in the *Thanks* section) for the answers to your prayers. I call this "my part" in prayer.

After I talk to God, I *listen* to him. I call this "God's part" in prayer. During this time, I meditate on Scripture, memorize important verses, review notes I've taken on sermons or Bible

Becky Tirabassi

lessons I attend, and read passages from the Old Testament, the New Testament, and Proverbs.

How important is it to have a quiet time with God every day? I believe that my quiet time has been the most important part of my growth as a Christian. Sure, it takes time and practice to get the most out of that time, just as it takes time and practice to become a better basketball player or dancer or piano player.

And it's important to keep it up regularly. I've kept my appointment with God every day for over ten years! Not only does it help me to know God better, but it's also where I've gotten *all* of my ideas for the books I've written and the videos I've made.

It should be obvious by now that, before I became a Christian, my life was a total mess. It wasn't just that I was breaking God's laws and hurting other people. The truth was, I was also very unhappy.

But when I became a Christian, an amazing thing happened. My whole lifestyle changed. For instance, because I'd been drinking so much, I was quite a bit overweight. After I became a Christian, I grew more concerned about physical fitness. I set a goal to eat right and exercise regularly.

Ever seen people walking around with pot

bellies or soft, flabby arms and legs? Lots of people get out of shape as they get older. Even those who were athletic when young can get too busy or too lazy to exercise and eat right after they've graduated from school and are working full time. That's understandable—but not very wise. Not taking care of yourself physically can lead to health problems, weight problems, and a poor self-image.

I didn't want to see that happen to me. Having been a cheerleader in school, I knew what it meant to be fit and trim—but by that time I'd also learned what it meant to struggle with being overweight. So I looked for a great way to exercise regularly, and I found one: I became an aerobics instructor!

For five years I taught aerobics in a Southern California health club, but the club never allowed me to do something I really wanted to do: play Christian music in my aerobics class. There was lots of great Christian music out there—why not work out to it? That way, we'd be reminded of one of the best reasons to stay physically fit—that our bodies belong to and represent God!

Lots of people get good, hard aerobic workouts at home in front of their VCR, using aerobics videos. But I looked around and discovered that there were no difficult aerobics videos made to hip-hop Christian music. So I prayed about it and asked God if I could make a Christian aerobics video. I prayed about the idea for almost two years. My first big break came when I was talking to a publisher friend, and he recommended that I see someone from Benson Music who was, in fact, only a few blocks away!

Once I'd made that contact, I started looking in earnest for a good choreographer—someone who could help me plan the moves and give my viewers a great workout. I had decided, by that time, that step aerobics—a system that uses a small platform onto which the user steps repeatedly during the exercises—provided the best aerobic workout. Through a series of conversations and answers to specific prayers, I heard of a possible choreographer, Candice Copeland-Brooks.

I first met Candice at a Reebok workshop being held only twenty minutes from my home. Upon entering the workout room, I saw over fifty fit aerobic instructors. I wasn't sure how I would recognize Candice. Then in the corner of the room, I spotted a petite, muscular, fair-skinned instructor who was eight months pregnant! Her black bike shorts and lacy leotard set off her pony-tailed, light blonde hair. Without a doubt, this was Candice Copeland-Brooks.

I was so nervous. But when I saw a chance to slip to the front of the room and introduce myself, I blurted out everything at once: "Hi, my name is Becky Tirabassi. Your friend suggested that I contact you about choreographing a Christian aerobics video. Would you be interested?"

"Umm," she replied, "just give my office a call."

I thought I had blown it. But in spite of my fears of being turned down, I called her office that week, and we chatted. She had everything that I needed: background, expertise, and experience. But she was expensive! Amazingly, though, she offered to cut her fee in half, and we began to work on the video.

From that day on, Candice went to the top of my prayer list. In our breaks from working out, we would talk. Little by little, I learned more about her. Someday, I hoped we could be friends. But I did not push myself on her.

The day of the shoot came. I flew to Nashville, and once there, I was pretty much a wreck. The rehearsals were grueling, but through it all my crew and I just kept praying. We prayed even over the little things: that a particular camera would work again and that

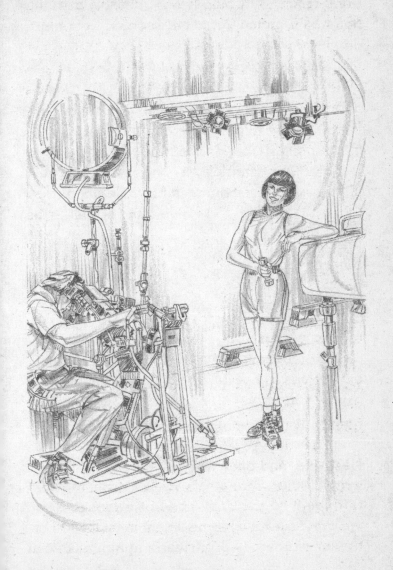

Spiritually and Physically Fit

Candice's baby would be comfortable with the hotel baby-sitter. And God seemed to smooth our way for us.

Once the shoot began, I was totally dependent on Candice for my every move. I was so nervous I kept forgetting whole parts of the routine. My only hope for getting through twenty-minute segments in one shot was to lip-read Candice and mimick her moves. She would point me to the left or the right, smile when I performed correctly, and guide me with her arms and legs.

By midnight, when we had completed the entire video shoot, I said, "I've never done so much lip-reading in one day."

Candice replied, "I've never had anyone lip-read as well as you!"

We laughed, but something had happened between us as a result of all that eye contact and trust. "You know," I said, "we've become soul mates!"

My words proved prophetic. A few months afterward, Candice told me she had accepted Christ. We *had* become soul mates—for eternity!

Our video, *Step into Fitness*, went on to win an Angel Award in 1992. It was also rated in the top nine for all the Christian and non-Christian

Becky Tirabassi

aerobic videos that were produced and reviewed that year!

The exciting response to my first video proved that a lot of people agreed with me: Great Christian music really *does* make a positive difference in your attitude when you work out. So why offer just one video? In 1993, I made another step aerobics video with Candice called *Thoroughly Fit*. We filmed it outdoors in Laguna Beach, California—not far from where I live.

This time, I decided that just a video wasn't enough. Together, Candice and I wrote a fitness journal called *Thoroughly Fit*. The book encourages people to balance their lives in four areas: spiritually, physically, emotionally, and mentally. I wanted to help people learn some of the lessons that I had learned—that you must be spiritually fit if you want the rest of your life to stay in balance. When you make God an important part of your day, have a healthy body, have good friends, get along with your family, and are learning and growing, you will be much happier!

Maybe you're saying, "But I'm just a kid. What can I do? Should I pray every day too? Isn't praying just for adults?"

No! Jesus wants *you* to talk to him—no matter how old you are. After all, you may have some problems or struggles, too. Maybe you don't have any good friends. Maybe you don't get along with your sister. Maybe you're flunking in school. No matter what your problem is, Jesus wants you to bring it to him. That's why he said, "Do not let your hearts be troubled. Trust in God; trust also in me" (John 14:1).

I realized too late in my life that drugs and alcohol wouldn't take away my problems—when I sobered up, the problems were still there. In fact, drugs and alcohol just made more trouble for me. They stole my dreams and ruined my reputation. I wouldn't want you to learn those hard lessons by making the same mistakes I made. I would rather that you learn from *my* poor choices and bad decisions, and save yourself from suffering their consequences. That's why I've written this book.

Take a minute and ask yourself some questions: Do you have trouble getting along with your family? Are your friends a bad influence on you? Are you making bad choices? Are you scared about the future?

If you answered yes to any of those questions, then I can suggest something that will make a drastic difference in your life, just as it did in mine. Turn your life over to God in a simple prayer, the same way I did in that church basement with Ralph that day.

Becky Tirabassi

That prayer will be only the beginning of your relationship with God. *Every day* he will be as close to you as a prayer and a Bible. You probably aren't as old yet as I was when I finally turned to God. Great! The younger you are when you ask Jesus to come into your heart, the better! That way, he can guide and direct you during the difficult years ahead.

10

Fulfilling My Dreams

June 1994.

It's a summer evening in my hometown, and there's a cool breeze blowing in from the lake. Feels great. Feels like a lot of summer evenings I've spent here, but this one is different. This one I'll never forget.

I'm walking across the football field in the huge stadium—being led across, actually, with my husband Roger and son Jacob, by one of the officials here at the Billy Graham Crusade. Soon it will be my turn to speak—just the thought makes my stomach turn in excitement and anticipation.

Thoughts are racing through my mind. Years ago, as a teenager in this same town, I was making some of the most foolish choices a person can make, endangering my life and risking my future. I was defying my parents, living only for myself, and I had turned my back against God. It was eighteen years ago, here in this very city, that I admitted I was an alcoholic. Now many of the people I hurt or disappointed will hear me tell the story of how God changed my life; some will hear it for the first time!

God is in the business of changing lives, and tonight I will stand before these people as proof. He can turn something bad into something—or someone—good. For all the dreams I threw away or lost, God tonight is giving me the chance to fulfill an even better dream. For all the people I hurt or embarrassed, God, tonight, is giving me a chance to heal those relationships.

There'll be television cameras, of course—like most Billy Graham crusades, this one will be broadcast nationwide. So I've already spent my time in the makeup artist's chair, being made "camera-ready." Knowing that millions of

Becky Tirabassi

people will be watching me on TV just adds to my nervousness.

We walk up the steps to the platform, and the official shows us to our chairs. "Just have a seat and try to relax," he says when he sees how nervous I am.

Relax. Sure.

Roger smiles reassuringly at me. He's already told me several times how proud he is— and how thankful to God for giving us this opportunity.

As the first song begins and the crusade gets underway, I look out over the vast crowd and know that family members and friends have come from all over—Charlotte, North Carolina; Washington, DC; Baltimore, Maryland; San Francisco and Newport Beach, California; and Grand Rapids, Michigan—to support and encourage me as I share my testimony. I smile as I think of the fun we'll have when all of them join me afterwards for the little party I've planned—a far cry from the parties I used to go to in this town twenty years ago.

Why me? I wonder. I was just one more kid with a drinking problem, one more kid who was rude to my parents, who lied to get what I wanted. Why did God choose to save me from my own destructive habits, give me a wonderful family, and let me have the desires of my heart?

Because you asked me to, comes the answer. And it's true. On that day in that church basement, I turned in my desperation toward God. And in his love and mercy he answered my cry. Not because I deserved it. But because he loved me—loved me enough to send his son Jesus to die for my mistakes. Loved me enough to forgive me and take me into his arms.

He'd have done the same for anyone who reached out to him.

He'll do the same for you.

"Becky Tirabassi!" the emcee announces.

The time has come. I stand up—will my shaking knees hold me?—and walk to the microphone.

Mostly I see the bright lights, but beyond them I can see the stands stretching away into the distance, filled with tens of thousands of people. I think of my old high-school friends, many of whom I had invited to hear me speak. *Lord, touch their hearts,* I pray. Although I won't find out about it until later, five of those friends will come down to the front to turn their lives over to God when Dr. Graham gives the invitation at the end of the service.

But I need to begin.

"I recently sat on an airplane next to a lawyer who asked me what I did for a living," I say. "I told him I was a Christian speaker. He said, 'So what do you speak about?' I said, 'Well, I talk about having a relationship with God rather than a religion.' "

The microphone carries my voice throughout the stadium, and it echoes back to me. As I get into my story, I start to relax.

"Eventually, I just got this lawyer mad. He swore at me loudly and said, 'I don't respect you.' I said, 'That was rude, and you should never swear at a lady. Please excuse me while I spend some time praying.' So I opened my Bible and began to write my prayers for one hour.

"When I was finished, I closed my Bible, and the lawyer said to me, 'What pain did you experience in your life that you would pray for one hour?' "

I pause. Tens of thousands of people are watching me, listening to me speak. Because of who I am? No. Because of what God has done for me—and is waiting to do for them.

"I said to the lawyer, 'I tried to tell you earlier: I have a relationship with God, not a religion.' And I told him this story . . ."